Celebrations in My World

HAPPY BIRTHDAY!

Robert
Walker

Crabtree Publishing Company

www.crabtreebooks.com

Crabtree Publishing Company
www.crabtreebooks.com

Author: Robert Walker
Series and project editor: Susan LaBella
Editor: Adrianna Morganelli
Proofreader: Reagan Miller
Photo research: Crystal Sikkens
Editorial director: Kathy Middleton
Design: Katherine Berti
Suzena Samuel (Q2AMEDIA)
**Production coordinator and
Prepress technician:** Katherine Berti

Photographs:
Alamy: Corbis Premium RF: page 28
Associated Press: page 31
Dreamstime: pages 12, 23
iStockPhoto: cover (main image), pages 4,
6, 10 (middle), 14, 30
Keystone Press: Willie J. Allen Jr.: page 29
Shutterstock: cover (background), pages 1,
7, 8, 9, 11, 13, 15, 16, 18, 19, 20, 21, 22,
24, 25, 26, 27
Wikipedia: Suyash: page 5; Gemsling: page 17

Library and Archives Canada Cataloguing in Publication

Walker, Robert, 1980-
Happy birthday! / Robert Walker.

(Celebrations in my world)
Includes index.
Issued also in an electronic format.
ISBN 978-0-7787-4927-1 (bound).--ISBN 978-0-7787-4934-9 (pbk.)

1. Birthdays--Juvenile literature. I. Title. II. Series:
Celebrations in my world

GT2430.W34 2010   j394.2   C2010-902753-1

Library of Congress Cataloging-in-Publication Data

Walker, Robert, 1980-
Happy birthday! / Robert Walker.
p. cm. -- (Celebrations in my world)
Includes index.
ISBN 978-0-7787-4934-9 (pbk. : alk. paper) -- ISBN 978-0-7787-4927-1
(reinforced library binding : alk. paper) -- ISBN 978-1-4271-9444-2
(electronic (pdf))
1. Birthdays--Juvenile literature. I. Title. II. Series.

GT2430.W34 2011
394.2--dc22
                                              2010016408

Crabtree Publishing Company

Printed in China/082010/AP20100512

www.crabtreebooks.com   1-800-387-7650

**Published in Canada
Crabtree Publishing**
616 Welland Ave.
St. Catharines, Ontario
L2M 5V6

**Published in the United States
Crabtree Publishing**
PMB 59051
350 Fifth Avenue, 59th Floor
New York, New York 10118

**Published in the United Kingdom
Crabtree Publishing**
Maritime House
Basin Road North, Hove
BN41 1WR

**Published in Australia
Crabtree Publishing**
386 Mt. Alexander Rd.
Ascot Vale (Melbourne)
VIC 3032

Contents

What Is a Birthday?

A birthday is the **annual** celebration of the day a person was born. Some birthday parties are held on the day a person was born—but not always.

- We were too young to remember our first birthdays, but there are usually a lot of photos that captured the event.

DID YOU KNOW?

In China, children eat very long noodles on their birthdays. The extra-long noodles represent a long life.

4

Guests at a birthday party can be family, friends, and classmates.

Birthdays can fall on a school or work day, so many people celebrate their birthdays several days before or after their actual birthday.

Most birthdays are celebrated with a party, including gifts, games, and food.

5

An Important Day

Birthday celebrations are important for many reasons. They show appreciation for a person. Some people celebrate special **milestones**. Milestone birthdays are special or important years.

● In North America, many teenage girls will have a special "sweet sixteen" party on their sixteenth birthday.

Age 16 is a special year because a person can learn to drive a car. At age 18, a person legally becomes an adult and can vote in an **election**. Some people also consider birthdays that end in zero to be milestones.

An 80th birthday is worth celebrating!

DID YOU KNOW?

The song "Happy Birthday to You" is over 100 years old!

History of the Birthday

There are many different stories about how birthday traditions started. Some people say birthday celebrations began thousands of years ago in ancient civilizations, such as Egypt.

Ancient people thought noisemakers scared away evil spirits on your birthday.

DID YOU KNOW?

Ancient Greeks used to make "birthday cakes" to celebrate the Moon. The cakes were round like the Moon, and candles were added to make them glow.

In ancient times, people celebrated their rulers' birthdays with parades, music, and speeches. Rulers received valuable gifts.

Another story says that evil spirits visited people on their birthdays each year. The **tradition** of blowing out candles on a birthday cake comes from this story. People blew out the candles in one breath to show the evil spirits how strong they were.

● Some people believed that the smoke from blowing out birthday candles took prayers and wishes up to the gods.

Birthday Symbols

A birthday cake is a popular birthday tradition. Birthday cakes can be made in many different sizes, shapes, and colors.

- **What is your favorite kind of birthday cake?**

Putting candles on the cake is also a birthday tradition. The person's age is often marked with the number of candles on the cake.

Other birthday symbols include cards, wrapped presents, birthday hats, and party favors.

In North America, a birthday party is not complete without balloons!

DID YOU KNOW?

A popular birthday game in North America is called "Rock, Paper, Scissors." In China they play a similar game called "Jan, Ken, Pon."

11

Birthday Treats

The menu at a birthday party is full of delicious foods and sweets. Popular birthday party foods include pizza, hot dogs, hamburgers, french fries, and sandwiches.

Many parents try to have some healthier foods on the birthday menu, such as fruits and vegetables.

DID YOU KNOW?

Canadian birthday cakes sometimes have a coin inside them. The child who gets the slice with the coin wins a prize.

The birthday cake is usually served last.
It is big enough so everyone gets a slice.
Most people prefer chocolate or vanilla cake,
but there are a lot of other kinds! Cakes are
made in different shapes, such as a football
or a cartoon character. Of course, no birthday
cake is complete without ice cream!

Every guest gets a slice
when the birthday cake
is cut into pieces.

Birthday Activities

Good food is not the only thing guests enjoy at a birthday party. Family and friends enjoy talking and laughing with each other. Some birthdays are held at places such as a bowling alley, swimming pool, or park. Guests then have many different games and activities to enjoy.

● A bowling alley is a fun place to hold a birthday party.

14

Many birthday parties have **entertainment**. Music, clowns, and magicians help make a party fun! Everyone sings "Happy Birthday to You." Then the birthday person blows out the candles on the cake and opens gifts. He or she makes sure to thank everyone!

Some parties have clowns to entertain guests.

DID YOU KNOW?

Birthdays in Russia will sometimes include the "clothesline game." Small gifts are hung from the line, and guests are blindfolded before trying to grab a gift for themselves.

15

Birthdays Around the World

People celebrate birthdays all over the world. But not everyone celebrates their birthdays in the same way. In Holland, families fly a "birthday flag" outside their homes to announce birthdays.

● The custom of sending birthday cards first began in England over 100 years ago.

DID YOU KNOW?

In Korea, many people only have a birthday party for their first birthdays. After that, they celebrate getting older every Chinese New Year.

In Argentina, guests celebrate the birthday person's age by gently tugging on the child's earlobe once for each year of their life.

Birthday party foods are different, too. In Ghana, children get a special breakfast treat called *oto*. *Oto* is a patty made of mashed sweet potatoes and eggs. In India, children enjoy a rice pudding called *dudh pakh*.

In Australia, "fairy bread," made of bread, butter, and candy sprinkles, is often served at birthday parties.

17

Planning a Birthday Party

It is time to plan a birthday party! First, there are invitations to send. If the party is a surprise, you must invite people without the guest of honor finding out!

- You can make and send your invitations using the computer.

Next, you need to plan a menu. What does the birthday person like to eat? Do any guests have food **allergies**? Where will you hold the party? Will it be at someone's house, or at a special location? Be sure the location is big enough for the number of people invited.

● Helping to make and decorate the food for the party can be a lot of fun.

19

Your Birthday

It is your birthday! Congratulations! This is your special day!

Open the door and greet guests as they arrive for your party.

DID YOU KNOW?

Many children in Ecuador are named after a saint. Instead of having birthday parties, children will have parties on the same days their saints are honored.

Remember though, it is important for your guests to enjoy themselves at your party. Be sure to greet everyone when they arrive. Thank them for coming to your party, and offer them something to eat or drink.

Make sure that all of your party guests get chances to play the different games and enjoy the entertainment. Most importantly, thank guests for their gifts as you unwrap each present. Thank everyone again for coming when the party is over.

Thanking guests for their gifts is very important.

21

Choosing a Gift

If you go to a birthday party, you will probably bring a present. Choosing a birthday gift for a friend or family member can be tricky.

You can save up your money and buy something special for your friend or family member.

DID YOU KNOW?

Some families celebrate a birthday by bringing the birthday boy or girl breakfast in bed.

You can make all sorts of neat birthday gifts yourself. You could ask your parents or teacher for ideas.

Take time to think about the person you are getting the gift for. What are his or her interests?

Make sure you pick a gift you think he or she would really like. You might want to make a gift. A mug or a picture frame you have decorated yourself can be a special present.

Going to a Party

How you behave at someone's birthday party is very important! When you arrive at the party, **congratulate** the birthday person on this important day.

Crackers are fun at any party!

DID YOU KNOW?

Popular party favors in North America are "crackers." These tubes have a prize inside. Children pull the ends to open the crackers, and hear a "popping" noise.

Be polite to the other guests. Say "please" and "thank you" when the food and drinks are served.

Be sure to wait your turn when it is time for games. It is important to remember that this is a special day for your friend or family member. Do your best to make sure that he or she enjoys the party.

- Good manners are important when you attend a party. Do not get upset if you do not get your way.

Fun and Games

Birthday party games are fun for everyone to play! If the party is indoors, musical chairs and "Duck, Duck, Goose" are great games to try. Arts and crafts are also very popular at birthday parties. Guests may enjoy making drawings, playing with modelling clay, and building things from **papier-mâché**.

Pin-the-tail-on-the-donkey is often played at birthday parties.

Treasure hunts, sack races, and hide-and-seek are great outdoor party games. Most birthday games need very little **equipment**, and allow everyone to play.

Taking a swing at a **piñata** filled with candy is a very popular birthday game.

DID YOU KNOW?

In Peru, a popular birthday party favor is a pin made especially for the event. Many kids will collect and keep the pins from the different parties they go to.

27

Birthdays at School

Many classrooms have small celebrations for students on their birthdays. If a child's birthday falls on a weekend, the class will celebrate on the Friday before.

Birthday parties at school can be a lot of fun!

DID YOU KNOW?

Candies shaped like vegetables and fruits are a popular birthday party treat in Brazil. They are brightly colored and very sweet.

School birthdays are a great way to get to know all your classmates better. Students can make birthday cards to give to their classmate. At some schools, the birthday boy or girl gets to pick a fun activity or game for the class to play. Sometimes, the birthday boy or girl will even bring in cupcakes or other treats to share with the class.

Some classrooms have special birthday hats that you get to wear on your birthday.

29

Special Birthdays

Birthdays can carry very special meanings. In the Jewish religion, when boys turn 13, they have a **Bar Mitzvah**. This celebration marks the age that a boy becomes an adult. This is a very special age for Jewish boys. They are given more responsibilities and treated more like adults.

● At a Bar Mitzvah, Jewish boys take part in a special religious **ceremony**.

Some birthdays are so important that they are celebrated by entire countries! The queen's birthday in the United Kingdom and President George Washington's birthday in the United States are both public holidays in their countries. The birthdays are celebrated country-wide with big parades and parties.

The American Village in Alabama celebrates Washington's Birthday by dressing up and having cake.

DID YOU KNOW?

The birthday song was written by a pair of sisters, Mildred and Patty Hill. Mildred was a school teacher, and Patty was a principal.

31

Glossary

allergy A negative reaction to certain foods

annual Takes place once every year

Bar Mitzvah A coming of age ceremony for Jewish boys who have turned 13 years old

ceremony A formal event performed on a special occasion

congratulate To praise someone

election An event when people vote for their choice

entertainment A performance or event for people to enjoy

equipment Items or supplies used to do things

milestone An important event or occasion in a person's life

papier-mâché Paper and glue that gets hard when it dries

piñata A decorated container filled with candy that kids break open with a stick

responsibility Something you are expected to do

tradition A belief or practice that people feel is important

Index